# The British
# Bear Caper

# The British Bear Caper

## Stacy Towle Morgan

### Illustrated by Pamela Querin

BETHANY HOUSE PUBLISHERS
MINNEAPOLIS, MINNESOTA 55438

Published by Bethany House Publishers
A Ministry of Bethany Fellowship, Inc.
11300 Hampshire Avenue South
Minneapolis, Minnesota 55438

Printed in the United States of America.

**Library of Congress Cataloging-in-Publication Data**

Morgan, Stacy Towle.
    The British bear caper / Stacy Towle Morgan.
        p. m . —(Ruby Slippers School ; 4)
    Summary: While visiting Oxford, England, on her ninth birthday, Hope makes new friends and dreams of acquiring a new teddy bear.
        [1. Oxford (England)—Fiction.  2. England—Fiction.
3. Teddy bears—Fiction.]  I. Title.  II. Series: Morgan, Stacy Towle. Ruby Slippers School ; 4.
PZ7.M82642Br     1996
[Fic]—dc20                                                    96–25228
ISBN 1–55661–603–1                                           CIP
                                                              AC

To Ellen, Reid, Leslie Ann, and Grace—
who will always hold the key
to the door of my heart.

STACY TOWLE MORGAN has been writing ever since she was eight, when she set up a typewriter in the closet of the room she shared with her sister. A graduate of Cedarville College and Western Kentucky University, Stacy has written many feature articles and several books for children. Stacy and her husband, Michael, make their home in Indiana, where she currently spends her days home-schooling their four school-aged children in their own Ruby Slippers School.

# Ruby Slippers School

9702

# Prologue

By now you probably know my name is Hope Vivian Brown. I live with my mom and dad and my little sister, Annie. My sister and I are homeschooled. That means that while other kids go somewhere to learn, we learn at home.

Of course, homeschooled or not, there's lots to learn everywhere. That's why I like to travel.

The last trip we took was to Oxford, England. On most trips something doesn't go right, but on this one everything went wrong! I guess things don't always go as planned. Maybe that's not such a bad lesson to learn. But just wait until you hear the whole story—you'll see what I mean.

# Chapter One

Hope, you need to turn your light off. It's after nine o'clock and we have to get up early tomorrow morning!"

I looked at the clock. Mom was right. It was already ten minutes past nine. But I was just getting to the best part of the book *The Lion, the Witch, and the Wardrobe*.

"Can I read just a few more pages, Mom? I'm at the best part."

I heard Dad's footsteps. I shoved the book into my drawer and turned my light off. Dad poked his head in.

"Just in the nick of time, Hope," he said.

"Dad?"

He came in and sat down on my bed. "Yes?"

"Haven't you ever wondered what it would be

like to find a secret door to something?"

"How about the secret door to sleep?"

"C'mon Dad. You know what I mean. A door to a place no one else has been to. You know, a way to another world."

"Well, if no one else has been there, it would be a pretty lonely world," he said. He gave me a quick kiss on my forehead.

"Dad!" I said, waiting for an answer.

He leaned over and pushed my nightstand drawer closed. "Oh, you mean a place like Narnia in the book you're reading."

"Yeah, kind of like Narnia."

"You might just have to settle for a good book. But that's the neat thing about books, Hope. A good book and a good imagination can take you just about anywhere." He took my hand. "How about we talk more about this in the morning? We have lots to do tomorrow before we meet Nana and Papa at the airport, you know."

I pulled my bear, Ellsworth, close to me. "I wish Mom were coming," I said.

"She's staying behind to help out next door. Mrs. Mullins is very sick right now. She could use some full-time care until her daughter comes to stay. Anyway, this will be a pretty short trip. And I'm sure you and Annie will love spending some time in Oxford with Nana and Papa while I work in London. Papa can't talk about anything else. It'll be his dream come true to tour the library there."

He tucked me in tight and kissed me again. "Who knows? Maybe you'll find what you're looking for in Oxford."

# Chapter Two

T here they are!" Dad said.

We ran down the airport hall to meet Nana and Papa. Annie was faster than the rest of us. We caught up a few seconds later.

"Oh. You two are *so* beautiful," Nana said. Her white hair glowed around her smiling face.

"It's so good to see you both," she went on. She held my face in her hands. "Hope, you're getting so big. I can't believe you're almost nine years old. Pretty soon, huh?"

I looked at Annie. "Not soon enough," I answered. Annie was nearly seven and a half. And even though I knew it was impossible, I was beginning to think she might catch up with me someday.

Dad and Papa were already busy making plans. "I made reservations at a bed-and-breakfast in Ox-

17

ford. The woman who owns it is the sister of a good friend. We'll stay there Monday and Tuesday. Then we'll meet you back in London on Wednesday morning. Does that sound OK?"

Dad put his hand on Papa's shoulder. "You sure that will give you enough time to tour the library there?"

"No one can ever spend too much time in the library!" Papa joked.

Papa loved books, just like I did. He even used to teach English at a college in Maine. Since he's also a little forgetful, we call him the absent-minded professor.

The person at the desk announced it was time to board the plane.

We showed our tickets to the attendant, then started down the walkway to the plane. I could hear the engine and smell the fuel.

"It really stinks in here," I said.

"Smells like London already," Dad joked. "Whenever I smell diesel fuel I think of all those double-decker buses in Trafalgar Square."

I couldn't wait to get there. The first thing I wanted to do was ride in the top of one of those red double-decker buses.

We filed into the plane. "Hope, you sit with me over here," Nana said. "Annie, you sit between Papa and your dad. On the way back, you and Hope will switch."

A whole trip with Nana to myself! I was so excited. I couldn't wait for the plane to leave. Annie didn't look too happy to be stuck with the men. But she would be the first to get the mints Papa kept in his pocket.

Just then, Papa stood up in his seat and banged his head on the luggage compartment. "Ow!"

"Edwin, what's the matter?" Nana asked.

"I just realized I must have left my trench coat in the waiting area. I'll have to run back and get it. I don't want to be left without a raincoat in England!"

"You don't have time. We're about to leave!" Nana said, sounding a little worried. "You'll just have to leave it behind."

But Papa was already heading up the aisle. "It'll only take me a minute. You wait here."

Nana shook her head and smiled. "We're on an airplane, for goodness' sake. Where does he think I'm going to go?"

I got up and moved across the aisle by Annie, then looked out the window.

"I miss Mom already," Annie said.

Dad put his arm around both of us. "This trip'll be great, girls. There's nothing like spending a little time alone with grandparents. I wish I'd had more time like this with mine."

At that moment, the jet way connecting the airport terminal to the plane started to move.

"We're leaving without Papa!" Annie yelled.

I glanced out of the window. "Look!"

There was Papa, standing at the end of the walk-way with his raincoat over his arm. He was as calm as could be. The jet way moved back toward the plane door. An attendant helped Papa hop into the plane.

A few seconds later, he came strolling down the aisle.

"All taken care of," he said. "Now we're all set to go!"

"Are you sure you haven't forgotten anything else, Edwin?" Nana asked.

He snapped his fingers. "Oh yes! I forgot to give Hope and Annie one of my world famous mints!" He reached into his coat pocket and took out a tin full of white mints. We each took one and hopped into our seats. It was going to be quite a trip!

"Now that we're all settled in, Hope," Nana said once I sat down. "I want to talk to you about your birthday. I was thinking that maybe we could take an afternoon in Oxford and do some shopping. What do you think you'd like?"

I thought for a minute. "Well, I know I need new clothes. And I always like books. But I was thinking . . . oh, I don't know. Maybe I'm getting too old for what I really want."

The engine noise grew loud as the plane started down the runway. I could hardly hear what Nana was saying.

"You can tell me what you really want," she shouted. "Your mom said you wanted a cat. Is that right?"

"Well, yes, I'd love a cat," I shouted back. "But I don't think we can buy one in England. What I'd really like—"

"What's that?" Nana yelled. The noise was really loud now.

"What I'd really like is a another teddy bear!" Just as I shouted the answer, the engines went quiet.

Everyone nearby leaned forward and stared at me. I wanted to crawl under the seat. My face felt hot.

Nana turned a little knob above me, and a cool stream of air hit my forehead.

She leaned close and spoke quietly. "Sweetheart, it's OK. Don't be embarrassed. You need to take a lesson from Papa. Nothing bothers him, and he embarrasses himself all the time!"

We both started to laugh.

"Now listen. Did you bring your bear?"

I unzipped my backpack and pulled Ellsworth out from the top.

Nana took him and straightened the fur around his ears. "He looks very loved," she said with a smile.

"I think I must have fifty bears at home," she said as she patted Ellsworth and handed him to me. "When I left, the Director was all upset because

22

Campy had stolen his bed when he wasn't looking."

Every time we visited Nana, she had some of her bears posed on the dining room table. Sometimes one would be in a little bed or standing by a chair or holding a pot of flowers. She liked to switch them around when we weren't looking, then ask us about them. "What do you think happened here?" she'd say. Then we'd make up a story to fit the scene.

"Well, Hope. If I can have fifty bears and be more than fifty years old, I don't see why you can't have two bears when you're almost nine!"

"Makes sense to me," I said.

"Then it's settled. When we get to Oxford, we'll find a good place to go bear hunting!"

# Chapter Three

Dad had planned for us to go straight to Oxford from London.

"It'll work out better this way," he said. "You and Annie can get settled in and do some extra sight-seeing before you meet me back here to go home."

I was pretty unhappy. "But, Dad, I wanted to ride on the double-decker buses in London!"

"Honey, they'll have lots of buses like that in Oxford. Believe me! Now, don't forget to have Nana and Papa call me when you get there. I'll see you in only a couple of days."

He kissed both of us goodbye. I felt a little scared about the whole thing. It's not that I didn't love being with Nana and Papa. It's just that I wasn't used to being with them alone—especially not in a strange country!

"We're all set, girls," Papa said in his cheery way. "Looks like it'll be just the four of us for a few days. We better get this luggage over to the train so we can skidaddle on to Oxford."

As we walked behind Papa, we noticed the belt of his raincoat. It was hanging off the luggage cart!

"Edwin! You're dragging that belt all over the dirty floor," Nana scolded.

Just then, the belt brushed through a puddle of melted ice cream.

"Gross!" Annie and I said at the same time.

Papa turned around. "Oh well. I'll just stop and rinse it off at a drinking fountain," he said. "I was thirsty anyway."

He picked up the coat. "Watch out!" I yelled. Nana's suitcase fell off the luggage rack.

"Oh dear," he said. "Let me fix this." He grabbed the suitcase by the handle.

"Edwin! It's going to fall!"

Sure enough, the luggage toppled off the cart like dominoes.

Nana took charge.

"You just clean the belt. I'll take care of this," she said.

Annie and I watched as Nana reorganized the suitcases.

Papa placed the damp belt on the top of the neat

little pile. Then we all headed for the train as if nothing had happened.

"Isn't it a beautiful day?" he said. "A great day for traveling!"

"Aren't we lucky to have our own little compartment?" Nana said once we all sat down in the train.

A door closed us into a private "booth," or compartment. Two facing bench seats were covered in soft, green material. Above each seat was a rack for suitcases.

Nana smiled at me when I didn't put my backpack up above right away.

"You can take Ellsworth out," she said. "Later, when he has a friend, he might like to stay in the backpack."

I put Ellsworth between Annie and me. I looked out of the window. I wanted to be in Oxford that minute, but Papa said the trip would take another hour.

*Trips are always like this*, I thought. *I'm always waiting for something*.

I pulled out my book.

"What are you reading?" Papa asked.

"I'm getting near the end of *The Lion, the Witch, and the Wardrobe*," I said.

"A wonderful book!" Papa said. "Did you know that the man who wrote that book lived in Oxford most of his life?"

I looked at the cover of the book. "C.S. Lewis? Really?" I said. "Do you think we could meet him?"

"Oh, he died over thirty years ago," Nana said. "But you've already met him, haven't you?"

"What do you mean?" I said.

"Well, the best way to get to know an author is through his books, don't you think?"

Before I knew it, an hour had passed. We were coming into Oxford! I looked out the window. The first thing I saw was a big, red double-decker bus.

"Papa, wake up! We need to catch that bus!" I said.

We grabbed our luggage and headed for the bus station next door. Papa and Nana followed.

Annie and I ran onto the bus. We headed straight up the stairs to get the first seats. From there I could see almost everything. I glanced over to the train we had just left.

"Annie, look! In the train!"

"Oh no!" she said.

She shouted down the top of the stairs. "Papa, your coat!"

We waited a long time for Papa—so long I was afraid the bus would leave without him. Finally he came up the stairs. "You won't believe what a nice man I met when I went back to get my coat. He's a professor at Oxford University. We got to talking about the Bodleian Library—"

Nana broke in. "Sorry to interrupt, but is this the right bus to get us to the bed-and-breakfast?"

"I have everything under control, dear." Papa winked, looking quickly for his map.

# Chapter Four

We pulled up right in front of the bed-and-breakfast.

"That was a great ride," Annie said.

"I know. I felt like we were going to hit the tops of the trees," I said. "I kept ducking my head every time we came near a branch!"

While we were unpacking our things and washing up, Papa went downstairs to talk with the owner, Sophia. She was a sister of Papa's childhood pen pal. Besides running the bed-and-breakfast, she took care of her three grandchildren: Ellen, ten; Vanessa, eight; and Nicholas, two. Everyone called Nicholas "Nickel" for short.

"Nickel gets into everything," Ellen explained. "I have to watch him very carefully."

"When you're unpacked, you must come on

down. We'll show you round," Vanessa said sweetly. "We are very excited about having guests our age!"

Papa came upstairs. "So, are we all settled in?"

"Am I right in thinking there isn't a bathroom in the room?" Nana asked.

"I believe it's down the hallway." He pointed out the door.

"You mean we have to travel down the hall at night to go to the bathroom?"

"Well, I wouldn't call it traveling," Papa said. "All you have to do is walk."

"In the middle of the night when I'm half asleep, I'd call it traveling," replied Nana. "I thought we'd at least have our own bathroom."

"Many bed-and-breakfasts don't have private bathrooms, dear."

There was a knock at the door. It was Ellen.

"Do come down and join us," she said. "We are just about to have a game of Monopoly. Do you play that at home?" she asked.

"Yes!" Annie and I said together. We looked at our grandparents hopefully.

Papa winked. "Go ahead, girls. We'll rest for a while. See you in about an hour."

"Let's go," Ellen said. I followed behind her beautiful thick blond hair. It bounced back and forth as she walked down the stairs.

"Let's go over the rules quickly," she said. "Each of you starts with 1,500 pounds. And if you land on

Mayfair, you'd better watch it. Vanessa gets mad as a March Hare if she doesn't get to buy that one."

"Wait a minute," I said. "Are you sure we're talking about Monopoly?"

"Of course," Ellen said. "See?"

She pointed to a board that looked like ours at home, but instead of Boardwalk and Park Place there were Mayfair and Park Lane. In fact, almost everything was different.

Annie and I laughed.

"If you call money 'pounds,' then what do you use when you weigh things?" I asked.

"Stones. I weigh four stones," Ellen said.

I guess we had a lot to learn about England!

During the game, Vanessa and Ellen told us their grandfather owned a toy store on High Street in Oxford.

"It's not a big one like the ones they have in London, but Grandfather sells teddy bears and collectibles," Vanessa said. Her English accent made her sound very grown-up.

"You're kidding!" I said. "Our Nana loves teddy bears. Your grandfather must be really wonderful!"

Both Vanessa and Ellen grew quiet.

"Your turn," Ellen said, handing me the dice.

"Did I say something wrong?" I asked. "I didn't mean to."

"It's not your fault," Vanessa said. "It's just that ever since our mummy and daddy died, Grandfather

33

seems so angry." She twisted her brown curls around her finger and looked at Ellen.

Ellen went on. "You see, our parents died in a car accident when Nickel was only a baby. Ever since then, we've lived with our grandmother and grandfather. I don't think Grandfather will ever be cheery again. He works at the toy store late into the night. The only person he really talks to is Nickel, and I don't think he understands much of what Grandfather says." She paused. "Maybe that's *why* he talks to him."

I didn't know what to say. "I'm really sorry. It must be hard to be without your parents."

"Yes, well, I guess we're in the same boat—for a few days, anyway," Ellen said. She smiled a little. "I think we shall get on quite nicely, don't you?"

*Crash!*

Annie and I followed Ellen and Vanessa to the back of the house. The top window in the back door was in tiny pieces.

Nickel stood with his face against the door.

"Nickel! What did you do?" asked Vanessa.

He grinned. "Nickel hit door hard!"

Just then, Mrs. Townsend walked in. "Dearie me, what's my little Nickel been up to now?"

"I think he broke the window with a stick," Vanessa said.

Mrs. Townsend opened the door and picked up

Nicholas. "You're a terror, my little one. But I love you just the same."

"As you can see, Grandmother is a bit soft on Nicholas," Ellen whispered to me.

"Just a bit," I replied with a giggle.

# Chapter Five

W hat was all that noise a few minutes ago?"
Nana said when she and Papa came down.
"Was someone hurt?"

"No, Nicholas broke a window," Annie said.
"Mrs. Townsend is cleaning it up."

"Oh dear!" Nana exclaimed.

Papa changed the subject. "Nana and I have
been talking. We've decided to invite all of you girls
to come with us for high tea at the Randolph Hotel."
He turned to Ellen and Vanessa. "I know it's not
something you get to do very often . . . probably
only when visitors come, right?"

Vanessa laughed. "It does seem that way. We
usually just get by with tea and scones."

"I'll tell you what," Nana said. "We hadn't
planned on it, but why don't we take Nicholas with

us? Your grandmother could probably use the break."

"Are you sure, Mr. and Mrs. Cole?" Ellen asked. "He's sure to be a bit difficult by this time in the afternoon."

"Oh, we're sure," Papa answered. "He can't do much to embarrass me!"

"I'll go talk to your grandmother," Nana said. "I'll help get Nickel freshened up, then we'll be on our way!"

Not long after that, Nana came into the front room holding Nicholas's hand.

"A-ready," he said.

"Oh, Mrs. Cole. Are you sure you want him to wear *that*?" Ellen asked, pointing to his all white outfit.

"Well, your grandmother insisted that if he was going to the Randolph Hotel, he must be dressed properly," she said.

Nicholas blew bubbles from his mouth. His red, curly hair was slicked back away from his face. He had on white shoes, white socks, white shorts, and a white shirt. The only thing that wasn't white was the light blue tie on his sailor suit.

"Shall we be going?" asked Papa.

The walk to the Randolph Hotel was too long for a two-year-old, so Papa paid for a taxi. "We wouldn't want Master Nicholas to have an accident before we even got there," he said.

We stepped out of the taxi right in front of the beautiful old hotel. We walked into the lobby, and Papa asked a host to set us up for high tea. But when the man returned, he told us the only place he had left was a round couch.

"I'd be happy to set up small tables for you there," he said, "but it might be a bit difficult with the children."

"Anything will be wonderful," Papa said. "I'm sure we'll manage just fine."

Nana frowned. I could tell she wasn't too sure this would work out.

"Edwin, I think it's going to be hard to keep track of Nicholas. He will want to crawl all around the couch."

But it was too late. Papa was already on his way to the couch.

The waiter brought our tea and placed it gently on the small tables in front of us.

"I'll show you the English way to pour a cup of tea," Ellen said. She held the cup daintily in one hand and the teapot in the other.

Nana got up and asked if anyone needed to go to the rest room. She was taking Annie and didn't want to have to make another trip.

I said I'd stay with Vanessa and Ellen. I glanced at Papa. Nickel was sitting very quietly next to him.

Everything seemed to be going well.

"Hope, would you like to go up and get our food?" Vanessa asked.

"I'll just tell Papa I'm going first," I said.

I turned to talk to Papa, but he was gone. So was Nicholas.

I let out a little squeal. "Papa!"

"I'm right over here, Hope," Papa waved from across the room. "Come over here, dear. I'd like you to meet the man I was telling you about. Remember the one I met when I had to go back on the train to get my raincoat?"

"It's nice to meet you, Mr. . . ." I stopped short. "Papa, do you have Nicholas?"

"Nicholas? Why, he was sitting very nicely on the other side of the couch from you. Right over . . . oh, dear, Mr. Semple. You'll have to excuse me."

Grandpa dashed to the couch. "Now, don't worry, Hope. We'll find Nicholas. We just better do it before your Nana gets back. She'll have my head!"

"Too late," I said. "Here she comes!"

"Where's Nicholas, Edwin?" Nana asked suspiciously.

Papa started to panic a little. "Well, Elise, I knew where he was a minute ago. . . ."

"Edwin! How could you! You lost a child?"

"He was sitting so quietly on the couch—"

Just then, we all heard Nicholas laugh.

"Did you hear that?" I asked. "Over by the table."

40

We all looked toward the big, round table in the middle of the room. On it was every sort of yummy food you could think of . . . silver bowls of whipped cream, tiny chocolate eclairs, frosted tea cakes, and crustless cucumber sandwiches.

Nicholas gurgled, "Got it, got it!"

He was under the table!

"No, Nickel!" we shouted, running for the table.

Nickel lifted the tablecloth and began to crawl out. Still on his knees, he gave the tablecloth a hard tug.

I didn't dare look!

When I opened my eyes, Nicholas stood there with a smile on his face and a pile of whipped cream on his curly red hair.

"All fall down," he said, landing on his bottom on the food-covered carpet.

Papa sighed and looked at the whipped cream dripping down Nicholas's face. "Oh, well. Look at the bright side," he said. "He's *still* all white."

# Chapter Six

I can't believe Nicholas managed to get nothing on him except whipped cream," Annie said as we headed out the door of the Randolph Hotel.

"And I can't believe how much that afternoon tea cost us," Nana said.

"The man at the desk said they were about to have the carpet cleaned anyway. I guess things worked out in the end," Papa said.

"Do you think we could walk back up High Street and see Mr. Townsend's toy store?" I asked. "It would save us taxi fare and give Nickel's hair a chance to dry."

Nicholas shook his head like a wet dog.

"Nicholas! Watch what you're doing!" Vanessa warned.

Nana and Papa agreed to stop at the store before

going home. "After all, it's getting close to closing time. We won't bother your grandfather for very long."

I held Nana's hand as we walked up the street. "Nana, did you know that Mr. Townsend owned a toy store that sells bears?"

"Not until Mrs. Townsend told me," Nana answered. "She also told me how difficult these past few years have been for him. She said he is still very angry about the accident that killed his daughter and son-in-law."

"But it wasn't anyone's fault, was it?"

"Actually, it was," Nana sad. "Mrs. Townsend told me that the children's parents were killed by a drunk driver."

"A drunk driver?" I said. "I don't understand why people think they can drive when they've been drinking alcohol."

"Well, neither does Mr. Townsend. And I'm not sure he'll ever forgive the driver or God for the way things turned out."

"What happened to the person who hit them? Did he go to jail?"

"That's what I wondered. Mrs. Townsend said that the man walked away with very little punishment. He found a way around the law. I think that's what makes the whole thing doubly hard."

Nana stopped and turned to me. "You know, Hope, the older you get, the harder it can be to forgive. People get set in their ways."

"Well, here we are," Papa said. "Nickel Toys."

I turned to Ellen. "I didn't know that your grandpa named his toy shop after Nicholas!"

"He didn't," she said. "He's a Nicholas, too."

A little bell rang when we walked in.

The store was kind of dark. As we walked down the narrow aisles, the floors creaked. It smelled musty and old. Most of the toys were made of wood. A bright light shone in back.

"That's where Grandfather keeps most of the bears," Vanessa whispered.

I followed Nana down three stairs into the back of the shop. The stairs opened into a room full of every kind of bear you could imagine. There were bears with short noses and long paws. Some were dressed in velvet, and some in plaid. Some had hats. I even saw a few with teeth! I walked over to one girl bear wearing a blue-and-white jumper and a little straw hat. I reached my hand out to touch her dress.

"Don't touch her frock!" came a booming voice from behind.

I nearly jumped out of my shoes.

"There's no need to scare her," Nana said, coming to my rescue.

I turned to see an old man who looked very much like St. Nicholas—a little fat and with a full white beard. His eyes, though, had no Santa Claus twinkle in them. They were very angry looking.

45

"I . . . I'm . . . sorry," I stammered. "I didn't mean to hurt anything."

"Humph! That's what all children say before they break something."

Nana stood between me and Ellen's grandfather. "I think it would be almost impossible for her to break a bear, Mr. Townsend."

"Who are you?" he asked gruffly.

"My name is Elise Cole, and my husband, Edwin, and I are staying at your bed-and-breakfast down the street. These are our grandchildren, Hope and Annie. They've been enjoying getting to know your grandchildren. In fact, we just got—"

Mr. Townsend broke in. "Don't they have any parents?"

"Why, yes, they do. Their father is on business in London, and their . . ."

He interrupted again. "Don't want to hear it. Where are the children? Are you here to leave them off?"

"Grandfather," Vanessa said. "They just came to look around and to meet you. Mrs. Cole especially loves bears. She collects them."

Mr. Townsend turned his back on Vanessa and started to straighten the bears on the top shelf. "I wouldn't love anything too much if I were you," he muttered.

"We're sorry to bother you. We'll just have a look around here and be off," Nana said. "You have the best selection of bears I've ever seen!"

I didn't want to be anywhere near Mr. Townsend right then. He was scary. I backed away and found my way back up the steps on one side of the shop. Most of the shelves here were stacked with wooden trucks and cars. *Nothing too interesting*, I thought.

I knelt down to look on the bottom shelf. My eyes rested on the cutest bear I had ever seen. He was sitting very straight in the seat of an old wooden car. He looked handsome in a cap and a vest. I looked around to make sure Mr. Townsend wasn't looking.

"What is your name?" I whispered. A crumpled tag hung on his right wrist. It read: *My name is Babbins*.

"Hello, Babbins," I said, shaking his paw. "My name is Hope. Are you out for a drive?"

I heard a noise and jumped back.

"Oh, it's just you, Nickel." I put Nickel on my lap and held him in front of the bear. "Do you know Babbins?" I asked.

"Babba," Nickel said.

"Isn't he just perfect? I'd give almost anything to have him," I said.

I put Nicholas down and went to get Nana. I showed her Babbins, too. "He's just what I want for my birthday," I said.

She looked him over carefully. "He *is* very cute," she said. "But he's also very expensive. They just don't make bears like this anymore.

"I'll tell you what. Let's leave him right where he is and think about it. If he's meant to be yours, he'll still be here tomorrow when we come back."

I gave Babbins one last look before we left the store.

"See you tomorrow—I hope."

# Chapter Seven

The next morning was cold and damp.

"Psst, Annie. Are you cold?"

"Not as cold as you are," she replied. "Your feet are freezing!"

"Well, I guess they're going to be colder in a minute. I need to get up and get dressed." I felt like you do right before you're going to jump into a cold swimming pool.

"It's now or never!" I said, throwing back the comforter and racing into my clothes.

"It sure doesn't feel like a June morning," I said.

When we got down to breakfast, Nickel had already managed to get jam on the tablecloth and tip over a glass of juice.

Vanessa and Ellen were cleaning it up.

"Have a seat right over there, Hope," Vanessa

said. "Grandmother will be with you in a minute."

Mrs. Townsend came out with a silver rack. On it were triangles of toast lined up like cards in their slots.

"We have eggs, sausages, broiled tomatoes for each of you, and spoonfuls of beans. Enjoy!" she said.

I sure wasn't used to beans and tomatoes for breakfast. They weren't too bad.

Papa suggested we go for a walk around town after breakfast. We'd stop for lunch at St. Aldate's Coffee Shop, then go punting.

"What's 'punting'?" Annie asked.

"Well, it's boating in a flat-bottom boat. But instead of rowing, you move along by sticking a long pole into the river bottom, then shoving off," Ellen explained. "You just have to be careful not to get stuck holding the pole when the boat moves out from under you."

"Then I think we'd better ask someone else to punt for us," Papa said. "I wouldn't want to fall in!"

So after breakfast, we headed out for our walking trip around Oxford. We decided to take Nickel with us in his stroller until after lunch.

"Why don't you drop him off at the toy store after lunch? I'll pick him up there," Mrs. Townsend suggested. "It's such a break for me to have you watch him for a few hours. I might even get some slipcovers made for the chairs downstairs!"

Annie and I couldn't wait to see all the sights! We had our backpacks so we could take along our notebooks.

Not long into the walk, we crossed a bridge. Papa stopped us. "This is the college where C.S. Lewis taught," Papa said.

"But I thought we were at Oxford University," I said. "Is it a college or a university?"

"That's a good question, Hope. You see, Oxford is made up of thirty-five colleges. Those colleges together make up Oxford University," he told us.

"So this is where C.S. Lewis wrote about Aslan and Lucy and Mr. Tumnus?"

I felt a shiver of excitement. "I wish I had been here when he was."

"Let's walk over to Blackwell's Bookstore," suggested Papa. "If the Bodleian is the largest library in the world, Blackwell's has got to be one of the biggest bookstores."

On the outside, Blackwell's sure didn't look like one of the biggest bookstores in the world.

Nana took me by the hand.

"The rest of you wait right here. I have a little errand to run with Hope."

We walked inside. The bookstore was filled to the ceiling with books. In the middle, the store opened into many levels of rooms. This was even better than a double-decker bus!

Nana led me to the section of C.S. Lewis books.

"Here," she said, taking a slim book down from a shelf. "I want to get this for you."

I read the title. "*C.S. Lewis's Letters to Children*." I hugged it close to me. "Thank you, Nana. This is perfect."

She took my hand. "Now, let's go pay for this and leave before we get lost in here!"

Out front on the sidewalk, Annie practically landed on me. "Whad'ya get?" she asked.

"Just a little book. I'll show you later."

Papa put Nickel back in the stroller. "We better hurry up and move on. While you were in the store, I walked over to the Bodleian. We'll be included in their last tour this afternoon before it closes. That should give us plenty of time for lunch and punting."

"I'm getting a bit hungry," Ellen said. "And I think Nickel's a bit restless. If we hurry, we can get back to St. Aldate's before the noontime rush."

We hurried down the streets full of buses and bicycles.

Along the stone walls of the colleges were giant wooden doors that were shut tight. Instead, people walked through mini doors not much taller than Nana.

"What are those?" I asked. "They look like secret doors."

"Those are just smaller doors into the colleges. They've been cut into the larger doors so the big doors can stay shut," Ellen said. "Most grown-ups have to bend down to even get through."

"You try it, Mr. Cole," Vanessa urged.

Papa bent down and walked through one of the open doors. When he came back through, he bumped his head. "Oops! I forgot. You really do have to be careful," he said, rubbing his forehead.

"Now you try it, Hope," he said.

I walked through with no trouble. "It's just the right size for me," I pointed out. "This is one time when it's nice to be short!"

All the way to the coffee shop, I kept looking at those doors. Maybe there really was a secret door to something in Oxford, just like Dad had said.

"If we finish our lunch early we might get a chance to hear the boys' choir practicing for the evening church service, Evensong," said Ellen.

We reached the coffee shop just as they were taking out the trays of food. While we waited, I bought a couple of candy bars and stuffed them into my backpack. "For later." I winked at Annie.

"They have wonderful soups, pasties, and hot dishes here," Vanessa said. "You might try a pasty since you probably don't have those in America."

"What are they?" Annie asked.

"They're meat and potatoes folded up in a sort of pie crust," Ellen explained. "They're really quite good. I think I'll share one with Nickel."

After lunch we hurried over to the church. When we walked into the building, we heard the sounds of

the pipe organ and the beautiful voices of the boys' choir.

"We got lucky," Vanessa said. "They don't often practice at this time of the day."

The music made me feel like I had just stepped into heaven.

Even Nicholas was hushed by the pretty sounds.

When I sat on a wooden bench, I could feel the low rumble of the organ through the wood.

I leaned over to Ellen. "It feels like God is right here in this building."

Ellen nodded, but she had a sad look on her face.

After a while, Papa led us out the door and into the gardens.

I was walking next to Ellen. "Is something wrong?"

"Kind of," she said. "When I was little, Mummy and Daddy used to take us to Evensong once a week. We would sit and listen to the men and boys' choir sing. I know Mum would want us to go to Evensong, but my grandparents don't let us. Sometimes I sneak into the practices just so I can hear them . . . so I can remember.

"Someday, maybe, Grandfather will learn how to forgive," Ellen said. "Then we can come to church together again as a family."

# Chapter Eight

When we dropped Nicholas off at Nickel Toys after lunch, Mr. Townsend wasn't too happy.

"I don't have anyone here at the store to help me. If Nickel gets into mischief, it won't be my fault," he said.

Nickel ran up to his grandfather and hugged his leg. Then he reached up and held out his arms. "Up," he said. "Up."

Mr. Townsend's face relaxed as he picked Nickel up. "You're a bad little tike, you are. I haven't got any use for you."

Nickel just smiled back and gave his grandfather a kiss.

We walked out of the store. I was glad to be outside. I was even more glad to have left my heavy backpack at the store.

Punting on the river was lots of fun, but I could tell Papa was getting anxious to go to the library. Nana looked tired. The warm sun and the big lunch we had eaten had worn all of us out.

"I'll tell you what, Elise," Papa said. "Why don't you and the girls go back to the bed-and-breakfast? I'll just go to the Bodleian Library alone."

"You're probably right, Edwin. A library tour might be a little much after such a long day. What do you say, girls?"

Annie and Vanessa were ready to go home, too. I wanted to go with Papa. Ellen said she'd join us. So we all walked back to the toy store so we could pick up our backpacks. While we were there, I also wanted to get one last look at Babbins.

But when we got back into the toy store, it was quiet. There was no sign of Mr. Townsend anywhere. I walked over to the far aisle to visit Babbins before Mr. Townsend showed up. I kneeled down where I remembered him being and gasped.

He was gone!

Just then, I turned and saw Mr. Townsend standing at the end of the aisle. "Looking for something?"

I quickly stood up. "Mr. Townsend, sir . . . I was . . . just . . ."

"You were just what? Looking for a truck or a car that you liked?"

"No, sir . . . I was just . . ."

Ellen appeared at the other end of the aisle.

"Grandfather, we were looking all over for you. Where were you?"

"I was right here all the time, Ellen," he said matter-of-factly. "What are you doing back here? Nickel has already gone home with your grandmother."

"Yes, we thought that he'd be gone by now. We just came by to get Hope and Annie's backpacks."

"Yours looks pretty full. What have you got in there?" Mr. Townsend asked. I felt like he was accusing me of something.

"Nothing much," I said. "Just some note pads and sketch pads and candy bars."

"Hmm . . ." he said. He looked down to where Babbins had been.

I wanted to ask him who had bought the bear, but I wasn't brave enough.

"Well, goodbye!" I said.

Ellen and I ran out of the shop and out onto the sidewalk.

Papa came out after us. "I think Nana is going to do a little bear shopping of her own while we head to the library."

The closer we got to the library, the faster Papa walked. "Hurry along, girls. Mr. Skelly, our tour guide, will be waiting for us at the entrance. Ah, there he is now." He waved at the man coming toward us.

Mr. Skelly spoke first. "Well, hullo, Ellen. You

were just toddling about when I met you the first time, but I'd remember you anywhere. Still have that beautiful blond hair, I see." He then turned to me. "And who is this, Mr. Cole?"

"This is my granddaughter Hope. Hope, this is Bob Skelly. He gives tours here at the library when he's not working there. He's the one who makes sure everyone gets the books they need."

"Well, I try anyway. Right now we're in between terms, so we can take as much time as we need. The biggest crowds we have to deal with this time of year are the tourists. Otherwise, the library is pretty much empty this week."

"They call Oxford the City of Great Spires," Mr. Skelly said. "Look around you and you'll see why."

I looked up. All around me, I could see the tall, pointed tops of the buildings.

We followed Mr. Skelly into the main building and joined a very large group of people who were waiting for the last tour. "If you happen to get separated from the rest of the group, catch up straight away," he said. "No one wants to be locked in the library."

Everyone laughed, and we started the tour.

Before long, Papa had inched his way to the front of the crowd. Ellen and I nudged ourselves past the others to get a peek at an original copy of one of William Shakespeare's plays.

"Can you imagine, Ellen?" I said. "This was

written in 1593. Over four hundred years ago. Wow!"

We stared into the glass case long after the last person walked past. "Uh-oh. Hurry! We'd better catch up with them," I said.

We ran around the corner and found the group. They were staring up at the beautiful ceiling. It kind of reminded me of the one in the church we had been to earlier.

"Did you ever notice how people whisper in libraries like they do in churches?" Ellen said.

"People don't whisper in my church at home," I said. "They shout!"

"Really? You're joking, aren't you?"

"Well, we don't exactly shout, I guess. But we do sing and worship more loudly than you do here."

"How?"

"Well, I guess nothing is as quiet at our church as it was today at the practice for Evensong."

"Quiet? Do you call the boys' choir and an organ at full blast quiet?"

"Well, no . . . I mean yes. It made me feel quiet inside. I liked it," I said.

At that moment, I realized it had gotten very quiet in the library. The group had left!

"Oh dear," I said. "I hope we haven't gotten lost."

Ellen was sure they had gone one way, and I was sure they had gone another. Since I was the visitor,

I let Ellen choose. But after a long while of searching, we still hadn't found the group.

It was starting to get dark, and we had seen nearly the whole library—or most of it. Two of the doors we tried were locked.

"Well, I don't know about you, but I have got to find a loo," Ellen said.

"A what?"

"A loo. A rest room, silly."

"Here's one," I said.

We walked in, and I looked out the window. "Oxford is beautiful from here. I can see the sun setting below all the buildings. And . . ." I stopped in the middle of the sentence. "And there's Papa and Mr. Skelly! They're leaving! They must think we already went home!"

I tried to open the windows, but they were locked. I banged on the glass, but they couldn't hear me from so far away.

Now I was really scared. Were we going to be locked up in this library all night? They'd have to come back for us tonight . . . wouldn't they?

# Chapter Nine

O nce they realize that we're not at home, they'll be back for us," Ellen promised. "We'll just find a spot to wait in one of the reading rooms."

I was glad she was a ten-year-old. She seemed a lot older right now.

"What have you got in that backpack? Anything useful?"

I remembered the candy bars I bought at the coffee shop. I reached over and started to unzip my backpack. "I can't think of anything better than a good book and a candy . . ."

I couldn't believe what my hands were feeling. This wasn't a candy bar. This was a teddy bear—and it wasn't Ellsworth! I pulled the bear out of my backpack.

Ellen gasped. "Babbins!"

"You know who this is?" I said.

"Of course, I do. He's one of Grandfather's favorites. But how did he get into your book bag?"

"I don't know," I said. "I honestly don't."

Ellen just stared at me.

"You don't think I stole him, do you? I would never steal anything! I don't do that kind of thing!"

Ellen's eyes softened. "I'm sorry. It's just . . . well, how *did* he get into your bag?"

"I don't know." I was getting worried now. "I don't know how any of this happened. And if *you* think that I stole him, what will your grandfather think? He's probably got the police looking for me."

"It'll be all right. Here, have a candy bar." Ellen unwrapped a piece and put it into my hand. "Someone will come soon, I bet. Anyway, we have Babbins to look after us, don't we?"

I took a bite of the candy bar. "You know, I used to think that getting locked up in a library would be a great thing. I never imagined it could really happen."

"Well, at least we have this flashlight. When they come back, we can flash it in the window. They'll be sure to see it.

"Meantime, let's look at the books around here." Ellen pulled one from the shelf. "Hmm. This looks interesting. *The Englishman and His Books*." Ellen opened the book, and a flurry of little yellow papers fell out.

"What is that?" I said, picking up a paper. "Shine the light so I can read it."

"It says, 'No volume or part may be taken away from one reading room to another without permission of the in-vig-i-la-tor'," Ellen read.

"What's an 'invigilator'?" I asked. "I think you better put that stuff away."

"It's all right. There are lots of books stored away in underground basements all through this area of Oxford. Someone has to keep track of them. That's what an invigilator does."

"Oh, great. Now I have to worry about an invigilator—or whatever you call it—running around the basement of the library!"

"Will you stop worrying! Mr. Skelly is an invigilator. It just means someone who works with the books in the library," Ellen said. "Speaking of books, don't you have that new book your Nana got you? Why don't we read that one?"

"Great idea!" I said. I opened up to page eight and started reading.

"Well, aren't you going to read it out loud?" Ellen asked after a minute.

I blushed. "Sorry. I got carried away. It says that when Clive—I guess that's his name—wasn't even two years old . . ."

"What's wrong, Hope? You're as white as a sheet."

"Ellen, look! It says here that C.S. Lewis's nickname was BABBINS!"

Ellen grabbed the book. "Let me see." She shut the book and looked at the teddy bear. "How odd."

Before I could grab Babbins, the flashlight beam went black.

"Ellen, turn the light back on," I said.

"I can't," she answered. "I believe it's lost its power. Now we're really in the dark."

I said a little prayer. "Jesus, please help us get out of here. And help Mr. Townsend not to be mad at me."

"I think I hear someone coming," Ellen piped up.

In the quiet library, it sounded more like an army coming. I started shaking. What if Mr. Townsend had sent the police after me?

"If we yell for help, they'll hear us," Ellen said.

"Help! Help!" we yelled.

Sure enough, a troop of policemen, or bobbies, came up the stairs and over to the corner. Nana was leading the pack.

"Oh, sweetie, I am so sorry! You must be so upset. I can't believe Papa could have let this happen."

I looked over my shoulder at Papa and gave him the OK sign.

"We were so worried about both of you," Nana said, taking our hands.

Papa came over and patted my head. "I'm sorry,

Hope. I thought you and Ellen must have gotten bored with the tour and gone home. I thought you left *me* in the library. I never imagined that I'd left *you*!"

"It's OK, Papa. It all worked out."

A bobby came up and shone a large light by us. "Let's get these things picked up and get down to the station." He picked up the bear. "Is this yours, miss?"

"Uh, yes. I mean no. . . ." I didn't know what to say. "*You* better keep it for now."

We started down the steps. Nana held my arm tightly. "Hope, I know you wanted that bear very badly. I also know you wouldn't steal to get something you want. How did that bear end up here?"

I wanted to find a door and run. "I don't know how it got into my backpack. You're the only one who knew about the bear. You, me, and . . ." All of a sudden, I thought of something.

"And Nickel! He knew I wanted that bear. I told him when he was sitting on my knee! You don't think Nickel put it in my backpack, do you?"

"There's only one way to find out!" Ellen said.

# Chapter Ten

When we got back to the house, the lights were still on. Mr. and Mrs. Townsend were sitting at the kitchen table. I was so scared to walk into the house that Papa almost had to drag me.

"Come on, now, you can do it. We're right behind you, Hope," he said. He tried to make me feel better, but it wasn't working.

The bobby came in ahead of me and handed Babbins to Mr. Townsend. "Here you go, sir. Now that we've returned your merchandise, do you prefer to let this young lady go?"

Mr. Townsend banged his hand on the table. "Absolutely not! I want this girl to pay for her crime. You can't steal things and then expect not to be punished. The law is the law."

Mrs. Townsend spoke up. "Nicholas, sit down.

Give Hope a chance to speak."

I swallowed hard. "Mr. Townsend, sir . . . I didn't steal your bear. I know it might look like I did, but I didn't." A tear rolled down my cheek. "You can't be so mean to people all the time. Why are you so mean, anyway? It isn't fair."

Mr. Townsend stood up. "Fair?" he asked. His voice was loud now. "Fair? Is it fair that I have no daughter and no son-in-law? What did I do to deserve that? I was a good man. I worked hard. I loved my family. I went to church and said my prayers. And what do I get? Nothing! I have nothing left!"

He sat down and put his head in his hands.

No one knew what to do.

Just then, Nicholas came in and toddled past the bobby, past Ellen, past Nana and Papa, and into his grandfather's lap. "Grandpa crying?" he asked. "Why Grandpa crying?"

Mr. Townsend held Nicholas close and began to sob—big sobs. The rest of us left for the front room.

The bobby spoke first. "I'll tell you what. Why don't I return in the morning? Sounds like Mr. Townsend has some things to work through."

Papa showed him out and came back into the front room. He sat down at the piano and started to play an old hymn. It was the same hymn he always played when he sat down at the piano.

I walked over to Ellen. "Do you think he's going to put me in jail?"

"I hope not," she replied. "I don't think so. Something's different tonight. Grandfather's never talked about Mummy and Daddy that way. I hope something's different, anyway."

Nana came and sat down next to me on the chair. "Hope, do you remember those little doors you walked through so easily this afternoon? Those doors to the colleges?"

"Yes," I said. "Why?"

"Well, I was just thinking about how easy it was for you children to walk through them. For the adults, it was much harder."

I tried to understand what Nana was saying.

"Tonight we've seen just how hard it is for Mr. Townsend to get past the hurt and anger he feels over the accident. It's like walking through those doors. A grown-up needs to bend to go through the door. Well, Mr. Townsend is going to have to bend a lot before he can get through the past. Give him time."

---

The next morning, we all came down to breakfast, knowing we were leaving for home soon. I couldn't wait to see Dad and Mom again. It had been a long trip!

Before we even sat down to eat, Mr. Townsend spoke up. "I'd like to say a few things before we eat."

He looked uncomfortable. "I want you to know that I plan to change some of the ways I have acted. Now, don't expect that it'll happen overnight, but I'm going to try to be better."

Mrs. Townsend smiled and started to clap, and then we all joined in . . . even little Nickel.

Mr. Townsend went on. "Now, about the bear. I talked to Nicholas last night. He told me that he put Babbins in Hope's backpack."

I let out a sigh of relief.

Nicholas sat in his booster chair clapping and saying, "Babbin. Babbin."

"As it stands," Mr. Townsend said, "it looks like I have some apologizing to do."

He walked over to where I was standing. It was hard for me to not be nervous. "Hope . . . will you forgive me?"

I couldn't believe it! Mr. Townsend asking for forgiveness! I looked up at him, smiled, and said, "I forgive you, Mr. Townsend. I'm sorry you've been sad for so long."

"So am I, Hope." He turned to the rest of the family. "I've wasted the last couple of years. I want to put things right. Tonight, we will all go to Evensong as a family." Ellen, Vanessa, and Mr. and Mrs. Townsend all hugged one another as little Nickel clapped and bounced in his booster chair.

"We wish we could join you, but we'll be on our way back to the States by then," Papa said warmly.

"We'll be thinking of you, though, won't we, Hope and Annie?" added Nana, squeezing my hand.

———

Once everything was packed, we said our good-byes. I promised Ellen and Vanessa I would write.

"Don't take Nickel to any more high teas at the Randolph," I joked.

"Don't worry," Vanessa said. "It will be a long time before they let him in again!"

"Well, I guess it's time we get going," Papa said. "Sophia, Nicholas, it's been a real joy to get to know you. I hope we'll see each other again soon."

I reached down to get my backpack, and Nicholas patted me on the back. "Babbins," he said clearly.

"No," I said. "Not this time, Nickel."

"Yes, Babbins," he insisted.

I took my pack off and reached inside. Sure enough, there was Babbins.

"Nickel!" I scolded. "You can't keep doing this." I started to hand the bear back to Mr. Townsend.

Mr. Townsend stopped me. "This time *I* did it," he said. "I want Babbins to go home with you where he belongs."

I gave Mr. Townsend a hug. "Oh, thank you so much!"

"Look inside his pocket!" Vanessa said.

Inside the vest pocket of the teddy bear was a little silver bear charm.

"It was supposed to be a secret," Ellen said. "We hoped you would find it later."

"I'm glad you told me now," I laughed. "I might have thought Nickel put it in there by accident!"

Just then the doorbell rang. Mrs. Townsend opened the door.

"It's the bobby," she said. "Come in, sir."

"I was just checking to see if everything turned out all right."

Mr. Townsend stepped forward. "Yes, sir. I believe everything is taken care of."

He looked back at me. "All is forgiven, right?"

"Right," I said. I couldn't tell if I saw a twinkle or a tear in his dark eyes.

The bobby stopped and looked at our luggage. "Can I give you a ride to the train station? It's the least I could do."

On the way there, we joked about the difference a few hours can make. "Yeah, last night you could have been headed for jail in this car," Annie said.

"I don't even want to think about it," I said.

We waved goodbye to the bobby as we boarded the train.

Once again, Annie and I sat facing Nana and Papa in our compartment. "Thank you, Nana and Papa. This has been a wonderful trip. We wouldn't trade it for anything," I said.

"It has been a wonderful trip, hasn't it?" Papa said. "All in all, it went pretty smoothly."

"I wouldn't go that far, Edwin," Nana chuckled.

The End

# Series for Young Readers*
# From Bethany House Publishers

★ ★ ★

## BACKPACK MYSTERIES
### by Mary Carpenter Reid

This excitement-filled mystery series follows the mishaps and adventures of Steff and Paulie Larson as they strive to help often-eccentric relatives crack their toughest cases.

★ ★ ★

## THE CUL-DE-SAC KIDS
### by Beverly Lewis

Each story in this lighthearted series features the hilarious antics and predicaments of nine endearing boys and girls who live on Blossom Hill Lane.

★ ★ ★

## RUBY SLIPPERS SCHOOL
### by Stacy Towle Morgan

Join the fun as home-schoolers Hope and Annie Brown visit fascinating countries and meet inspiring Christians from around the world!

★ ★ ★

## THE THREE COUSINS DETECTIVE CLUB™
### by Elspeth Campbell Murphy

Famous detective cousins Timothy, Titus, and Sarah-Jane learn compelling Scripture-based truths while finding—and solving—intriguing mysteries.

\* (ages 7–10)